Making Music

Heather Hammonds

Contents

Chapter 1

Music for Everyone

Everyone likes music.

We can listen to music.
We can play music too.

Music can be played by one person or by lots of people.

Music can be played on **musical instruments.**

These ***musical notes*** *are played on musical instruments.*

Chapter 2

Music from Strings

Some musical instruments have strings.

Music comes from the strings
when the musical instruments are played.

This boy is playing the guitar.
His **music teacher** is showing him what to do.

This guitar has six strings.

This musical instrument has strings too. It is much smaller than a guitar.

violin

All these musical instruments have strings.

Did you know that a piano has strings inside it?

Chapter 3

Music from Air

Some musical instruments are played by blowing air into them.

panpipes

This boy is playing the recorder. He makes high or low sounds by blowing into the recorder and pressing the little holes on it.

These very old recorders were made long ago.

This musical instrument is played by blowing into it.

The **musician** holds it to the side when he is playing it.

flute

All these musical instruments are played by blowing into them.

Some are big and some are small.

*These musical instruments are called **woodwind** instruments.*

flute

Chapter 4

Big Brass Sounds

Look at the musical instruments in this **marching band**.

The marching band plays music as it marches along.

This boy is playing the trumpet.
The trumpet is very noisy!

*These musical instruments are called **brass** instruments.*

tuba

Part of this musical instrument slides in and out when it is played.

This brass instrument is very big and heavy. Sometimes the musician sits down to play it.

tuba

Here are some more brass instruments.

French horn

trumpet

Brass instruments are played by blowing air into them.

Chapter 5

Taps and Beats

Some musical instruments are played with sticks,

glockenspiel

bongos

or with your hands,

cymbals

or by hitting them together.

This girl is playing the drums.
She plays the drums with **drumsticks**.

This big drum goes "boom-boom" when it is played!

This musical instrument
is played with sticks.
The musician hits the little bars
with the sticks.

These musical instruments make lots of sounds.
Have you ever played any of them?

You can play the drums with these special brushes.

Chapter 6

Playing Together

When lots of musical instruments are played together, they sound very good!

These children play in a band. They like to play music together.

Lots of people are playing musical instruments in this **orchestra**.

Everyone has a special place in the orchestra.

The ***conductor*** *helps the orchestra to play together.*

Chapter 7

A World of Music

Music is played all over the world with lots of musical instruments.

mandolin

bagpipes

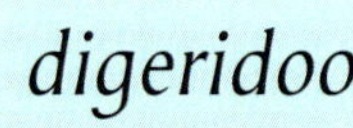

digeridoo

We can buy musical instruments.
We can make musical instruments.

We can make music by singing too!
Singing together is fun.

Glossary

brass a kind of metal

conductor a person who tells the players in an orchestra what to do

drumsticks sticks for playing the drums

marching band a group of people who play musical instruments as they march along

music teacher a person who teaches music

musical instruments special tools that play music

musical notes special kinds of writing that show different musical sounds

musician a person who plays music

orchestra a large group of people who play musical instruments together

woodwind a kind of instrument that may be made of wood and is played by blowing air into it

Index